Whooo... Has a Guide Inside?

http://www.ed-talks.com

ISBN-13: 978-1979235624
ISBN-10: 1979235627
LCCN: 2017917023

CreateSpace Independent Publishing Platform (a subsidiary of Amazon.com)
Charleston, SC

First Printing, 2018
Printed in the United States of America

This book was created by:
Christa Campsall (original concept, animal research, project coordination)
Jane Tucker (poetic interpretation of original concept)
Josephine Aucoin (cover illustration)
Gerardine Charlton (dream watercolor)

Stock images: Shutterstock
Young helpers: Ryleh, Fenwick, Johan, Frieda and Friends

Christa and Jane are residents of Salt Spring Island, BC Canada, which you may recognize as the setting of the story. Josephine created the "dog" and "Salt Spring scene" watercolors. She grew up on Salt Spring Island and Christa was one of her school teachers.

Whooo... Has a Guide Inside?

Two owlets looked up at the sky so blue.

They listened as Mama asked, "Who, who, *whooo?*
Who wants to leave the nest? Fly from our tree?"

"Not me!" said the owlets. "Not me! Not me!"

"One day you'll be ready; one day you will fly,"
their Mama laughed gently, eyes scanning the sky.
"We help and encourage our babies, it's true,
But the knowing of flying lies inside of you."

"But how can we know?" asked wee Hooty and Peep.

"It's a mystery! But you have wisdom so deep,
It will guide you forever, each step of the way;
give you courage to practice, and then, fly away!"

"Who, *whooo* ...?" asked the owlets,
"*Whooo* else has a guide?"

"Why everyone, sweethearts! We all do, inside!
Though all creatures are different,
there's something the same,
a one-ness among us, whatever our name.
Whether insect, or mammal, or bird in the sky
or swimmer of oceans, we each have a guide!"

"Let's look at our neighbours from mountain to sea
and ask them how wisdom inspires them to be!"

"And speaking of *beeee* … Here are three that I see!
Is there something you have to tell me, honey bee?"

"I'm a scout! I fly out and find nectar so sweet,
Then fly back to the hive where I share the sweet treat.
I dance for my friends, and my dance lets them know
The direction I came from, and how far to go."

"Hello busy squirrel! How are you today?
How does wisdom guide you as you work and you play?"

"I know to store nuts and seeds all around
and trust that I'll find them when snow's on the ground.
In winter, food's scarce, but I have what I need
all stored up and waiting, my family to feed!"

"Oh beautiful heron, standing so still,
what does your wisdom tell you?
Please share, if you will!"

"I know ... to be patient, to watch and to wait,
To fish for my dinner, and nest with my mate.
I have secrets to share, if one wishes to hear.
If you listen in calmness, your answer comes clear."

"Wild, leaping dolphin, at play in the sea,
What is it that guides you? Please tell Peep and me!"

"We dolphins are caring, we naturally give.
We rescue those injured, so that they may live.
Animals, whales, even people we save,
We lift them and carry them over each wave.

"Great powerful horses, oh how you can go!
Please tell us about you—something we don't know!"

"You might not know horses are rarely alone
We gather in herds so we feel right at home.
We see in each other the feelings we feel
'cause the looks on our faces, our feelings reveal!"

"Hello friendly dog! You look gentle and kind.
Tell us how you're guided, if you wouldn't mind!"

"I love to love people, and people love me.
Many feel I am part of their own family.
No matter what 'ups' and what 'downs' come along,
My heart keeps on loving, it's steady and strong."

"*Oooh* look! Over there, I see children at play.
Whooo are you? What's guiding you?
Please will you say?"

"I am me! I am me! I am happy to be.
I have wisdom and laughter and love inside me!
I can choose how I see life! I make my own day.
I can smile if I want, even when clouds are gray."

"I'm a dreamer! I dream and I watch dreams come true. Are you dreaming of me? I am dreaming of you!"

"Like the 'Circle of Life', like the moon, stars and sun…
I am part of it all, and so is everyone!"

"And like all those you've met, from mountain to sea,
There's a wisdom within, Love's true guide, inside me."

"Now we know *whooo* ... Who has wisdom inside:
Everyone! It's a gift—it's our own inner guide."

"We don't have to worry, for Love knows the way,
We're ready to fly! Up, up and away!"

Acknowledgement

As author, teacher and friend, the late Sydney Banks shared the fact that wisdom unfolds from within and is always available to guide us; it is truly who we are.

He helped people know and trust their own beautiful feelings of peace, love and joy, changing many thousands of lives for the better.

This poem was inspired by what we learned from Mr. Banks. We are profoundly grateful that the message of hope he shared continues to spread throughout the world. Mr. Banks lived on Salt Spring for many, many years. He loved the animals and the natural beauty of the island.

sydneybanks.org

Made in the USA
Columbia, SC
27 June 2018